BATAVIA PUBLIC LIBRARY DISTRICT

3 6173 00036 2882

D1404023

93-03098

jp
AYL   13.95
    Aylesworth, Jim

The Cat & the fiddle & more.

Batavia Public Library
335 West Wilson
Batavia, Il 60510
879-1393

Library Charges For
Missing Date Card

GAYLORD

BATAVIA LIBRARY DISTRICT
BATAVIA, ILLINOIS

NATIONAL LIBRARY BINDERY
BATAVIA, ILLINOIS

The CaT & the Fiddle & More

Atheneum • 1992 • New York

Maxwell Macmillan Canada
Toronto

Maxwell Macmillan International
New York Oxford Singapore Sydney

JP

93-03098

The CaT & the Fiddle & More

by
Jim Aylesworth
illustrated by
Richard Hull

Text copyright © 1992 by Jim Aylesworth
Illustrations copyright © 1992 by Richard Hull

All rights reserved. No part of this book may be reproduced or transmitted
in any form or by any means, electronic or mechanical,
including photocopying, recording, or by any information storage and
retrieval system, without permission in writing from the Publisher.

Atheneum
Macmillan Publishing Company
866 Third Avenue
New York, NY 10022

Maxwell Macmillan Canada, Inc.
1200 Eglinton Avenue East
Suite 200
Don Mills, Ontario M3C 3N1

Macmillan Publishing Company is part of
the Maxwell Communication Group of Companies.

First edition

Printed in Hong Kong by South China Printing Company (1988) Ltd.

10 9 8 7 6 5 4 3 2 1

The text of this book is set in Clarendon Light.

Library of Congress Cataloging-in-Publication Data
Aylesworth, Jim.
The cat and the fiddle and more / by Jim Aylesworth: illustrated
by Richard Hull.—1st ed.
p.   cm.
Summary: Presents new variations on the traditional rhyme "Hey
Diddle Diddle."
ISBN 0-689-31715-8
1. Nursery rhymes. American.   2. Children's poetry. American.
[1. Nursery rhymes.   2. American poetry.] I. Hull. Richard. 1945-
ill.   II. Title.
PZ8.3.A95Mo   1992
811'.54—dc20   91-30956

To Mother Goose, with love!
—J. A.

To my mother
—R. H.

Hey diddle diddle!
The cat and the fiddle,
The cow jumped over the moon;
The little dog laughed
To see such sport,
And the dish ran away with the spoon.

Hey fetter fetter!
The swan wore a sweater,
The fox hopped 'round on one paw;
The little lamb laughed
To see such sport,
And the board ran away with the saw.

Hey trifle trifle!
The sheep shot a rifle,
The goose tried hatching a rock;
The little calf laughed
To see such sport,
And the key ran away with the lock.

Hey sunny sunny!
The bear spilled the honey,
The mule did a two-legged trot;
The little rabbit laughed
To see such sport,
And the pan ran away with the pot.

Hey mango mango!
The pig danced a tango,
The owl ate the cornmeal mush;
The little girl laughed
To see such sport,
And the comb ran away with the brush.

Hey tapple tapple!
The turkey pecked an apple,
The rat played a new brass flute;
The little worm laughed
To see such sport,
And the sock ran away with the boot.

Hey daffy daffy!
The deer pulled the taffy,
The weasel gave a very sly wink;
The little lizard laughed
To see such sport,
And the tub ran away with the sink.

Hey redder redder!
The mouse nibbled cheddar,
The old ox carried a cane;
The little colt laughed
To see such sport,
And the rope ran away with the chain.

Hey thistle thistle!
The wolf learned to whistle,
The rooster sang silly songs;
The little snake laughed
To see such sport,
And the poker ran away with the tongs.

Hey holler holler!
The possum found a dollar,
The duck quacked her merriest quacks;
The little mole laughed
To see such sport,
And the log ran away with the ax.

Hey bower bower!
The horse picked a flower,
The turtle leaped high in the air;
The little squirrel laughed
To see such sport,
And the table ran away with the chair.

Hey Dinah Dinah!
The bull broke the china,
The coon plucked an old banjo;
The little bee laughed
To see such sport,
And the rake ran away with the hoe.

Hey gravy gravy!
The ram joined the navy,
The skunk sprayed French perfume;
The little hen laughed
To see such sport,
And the mop ran away with the broom.

Hey nuzzle nuzzle!
These rhymes were a puzzle,
A game I simply adore;
And if you laughed
To hear such sport,
Why don't you run, make up some more?